Dear Parent:
Your child's love of reading starts here!

Every child learns to read in a different way and at his or her own speed. You can help your young reader improve and become more confident by encouraging his or her own interests and abilities. You can also guide your child's spiritual development by reading stories with biblical values and Bible stories, like I Can Read! books published by Zonderkidz. From books your child reads with you to the first books he or she reads alone, there are I Can Read! books for every stage of reading:

SHARED READING
Basic language, word repetition, and whimsical illustrations, ideal for sharing with your emergent reader.

BEGINNING READING
Short sentences, familiar words, and simple concepts for children eager to read on their own.

READING WITH HELP
Engaging stories, longer sentences, and language play for developing readers.

READING ALONE
Complex plots, challenging vocabulary, and high-interest topics for the independent reader.

ADVANCED READING
Short paragraphs, chapters, and exciting themes for the perfect bridge to chapter books.

I Can Read! books have introduced children to the joy of reading since 1957. Featuring award-winning authors and illustrators and a fabulous cast of beloved characters, I Can Read! books set the standard for beginning readers.

A lifetime of discovery begins with the magical words "I Can Read!"

Visit www.icanread.com for information on enriching your child's reading experience.
Visit www.zonderkidz.com for more Zonderkidz I Can Read! titles.

Do not follow the crowd
when they do what is wrong.
— Exodus 23:2 NIrV

ZONDERKIDZ

Larry Makes a Choice
©2013 Big Idea Entertainment, LLC. VEGGIETALES®, character names, likenesses and
other indicia are trademarks of and copyrighted by Big Idea Entertainment, LLC. All
rights reserved.
Illustrations ©2011 by Big Idea Entertainment, LLC.

This title is also available as a Zondervan ebook.
Visit www.zondervan/ebooks.

Requests for information should be addressed to:

Zonderkidz, 3900 Sparks Drive, Grand Rapids, Michigan 49546

Library of Congress Cataloging-in-Publication Data

Poth, Karen.
       Larry makes a choice / Karen Poth.
           pages cm. — (I can read) (Zonderkidz veggietales)
         ISBN 978-0-310-74168-8 (softcover)
         I. VeggieTales (Television program) II. Title.
       PZ7.P83975Lad 2014
       [E] —dc23   2013034798

Zonderkidz is a trademark of Zondervan.

Editor: Mary Hassinger
Art direction: Karen Poth
Cover design: Karen Poth
Interior design: Ron Eddy

Printed in China

14 15 16 17 18 19 /DSC/ 13 12 11 10 9 8 7 6 5 4 3 2

I Can Read!

BEGINNING READING

1

Larry Makes a Choice

story by Karen Poth

"Cowboy Larry!" Sheriff Bob said.

"It's your turn."

Larry was excited.

Today was the Cattle Drive test!

"To pass the test you have to lead
100 cows over the mountain,"
Bob said.

"You can't go through the canyon,"
Bob said as they went outside.
"You have to go over the mountain."
The Scallion Brothers went too.

It was a VERY hot day!

"We'll need sunscreen,"

Bill Scallion said.

He squirted Larry's nose.

Bill didn't want ANYONE
to get sunburned.
He put shirts and sunglasses
on the cows too.

"Are you fellas ready?"
Sheriff Bob asked.

"Yee Haw!" Larry yelled.

"We are ready!"

The three cowboys began
their journey.
Bill rode in front.
Larry rode behind him.

Before long, Bill stopped.

"Let's go through the canyon,"

Bill said.

"It's shorter."

Larry knew it was wrong.
Sheriff Bob said to go
OVER the mountain.

MOUNTAIN
PASS

"Well," Larry said, "if they are going, I guess I will go too." Larry didn't want the Scallions to make fun of him.

The cowboys headed for
Dodgeball Canyon—
a very dangerous place.

Larry was worried.

"Let's go!" Butch Scallion yelled.

The Scallions weren't worried.

As they went farther,
Larry got more worried.

"We should turn around,"
Larry said to Bill and Butch.
The cows were a little worried too.

But Bill and Butch
didn't listen.
They kept riding.

"Come on,"
Bill called.
"Are you scared?"

Then, Larry changed his mind.

Cowboy Larry turned around.

"God doesn't want us to cheat," Larry said.

Butch and Bill laughed.
"We'll get there faster,"
they said.

But the cows weren't laughing.

They heard an odd noise.

BBBBOOOIIIINNNNGGG!

Suddenly, red dodge balls bounced
down the canyon walls!

Avalanche!

The cows escaped just in time.

Bill and Butch were in trouble!

Larry was on the mountain.

He heard the dodge balls bouncing.

He heard the brothers yelling.

Cowboy Larry galloped
back down the mountain.

He threw a rope
to Bill and Butch.
Cowboy Larry
saved the day!

When the cowboys got back to town,
Miss Kitty met with Bob
and Cowboy Larry.

"Well done, Cowboy Larry,"
Bob said. "You are a hero!"
Then they all had a cold
root beer.

The sun set.

It had been a good day.

Butch thanked Larry.

And gave him some moonscreen.